O9-AIG-326

Kitty Cat, Kitty Cat,
Are You Going To School?

BY **Bill Martin Jr and Michael Sampson**

ILLUSTRATED BY **Laura J. Bryant**

SCHOLASTIC INC.

No part of this publication may be reproduced, stored in a retrieval system, or transmitted in any form or by any means, electronic, mechanical, photocopying, recording, or otherwise, without written permission of the publisher.
For information about permission to reproduce selections from this book, go to www.apub.com/contact/permissions.

ISBN 978-0-545-78242-5

Text copyright © 2013 Michael Sampson and Bill Martin Jr.
Illustrations copyright © 2013 Laura J. Bryant. Published in the United States by Amazon Publishing, 2013. This edition made possible under a license arrangement originating with Amazon Publishing, www.apub.com. All rights reserved. Published by Scholastic Inc., 557 Broadway, New York, NY 10012, by arrangement with Amazon Children's Publishing. SCHOLASTIC and associated logos are trademarks and/or registered trademarks of Scholastic Inc.

12 11 10 9   21 22 23 24/0

Printed in the U.S.A.   40

First Scholastic printing, September 2014

The illustrations are rendered in watercolor paints and colored pencils on Strathmore paper.
Book design by Vera Soki
Editor: Margery Cuyler

To my grandson, Rhett Sampson
—M.S.

To my brother Tom and his wonderful family
—L.J.B.

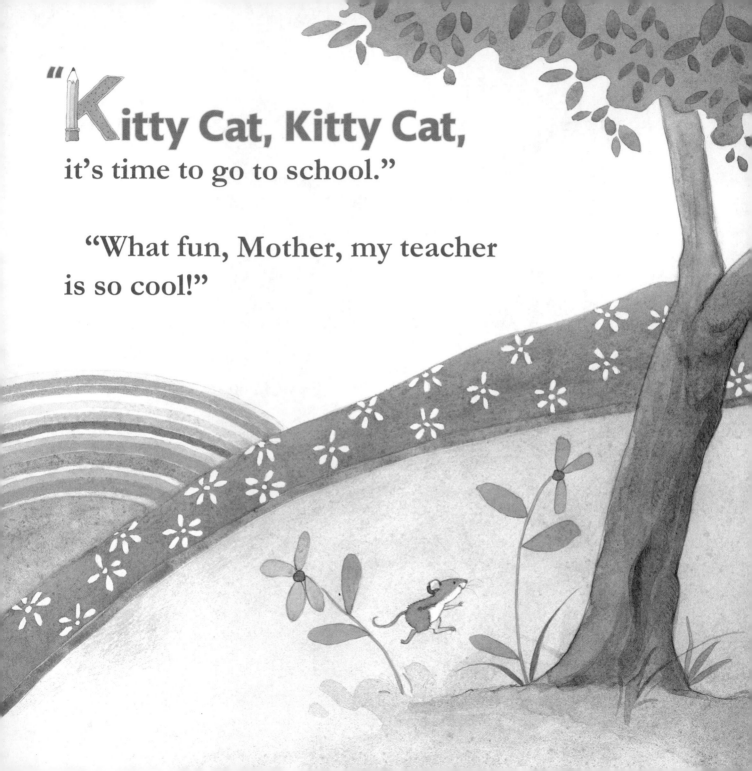

"**Kitty Cat, Kitty Cat,**
it's time to go to school."

"What fun, Mother, my teacher
is so cool!"

"Kitty Cat, Kitty Cat,
come sing a little song."

"Okay, Teacher, I like
to sing along."

"Kitty Cat, Kitty Cat,
let's open up this book."

"What fun, Teacher. I
see a monkey, look!"

"Kitty Cat, Kitty Cat, can you count to ten?"

"Oh, yes, Teacher, and back to one again."

"Kitty Cat, Kitty Cat,
go outside and play."

"Yippee, Teacher, my
favorite time of day."

"Kitty Cat, Kitty cat,
time to have a treat."

"Yum yum, Teacher,
I always like to eat."

"Kitty Cat, Kitty Cat,
you need to take a nap."

"Oh, yawn, Teacher, I'll
curl up in your lap."

"Kitty Cat, Kitty Cat, what's your show-and-tell?"

"Look, look, Teacher, I brought a little bell."

"Kitty Cat, Kitty Cat,
now it's time for art."

"That's great, Teacher,
I think I'll paint a heart!"

"Kitty Cat, Kitty Cat, your day at school is done."

"Yes, yes, Teacher, and I had SO MUCH FUN!"